THE CHRISTMAS GRANDMA RAN AWAY FROM HOME

INCLUDES GRANDMA CATCHES A WAVE

NANCY WARREN

AMBLESIDE PUBLISHING

INTRODUCTION

The Christmas Grandma Ran Away from Home

Long time widow Sandy Forbes is breaking out this Christmas. In her 71 years on earth she has stuffed and cooked 55 Christmas turkeys, baked hundred hundreds pies, turned out thousands of shortbread cookies and hoisted enough pine trees in her living room to reforest the Amazon.

Her family love her. They come to her for every occasion, eating, drinking, squabbling and then leaving her with a mass of dishes and crumpled holiday wrap. But this is the year everything changes. When she wants someone else to take over for one year, the family lays a big guilt trip on her and Grandma rebels. Sandy's giving herself a gift this Christmas. She's running away from home for the holidays.

"I'm not cooking a turkey this year," Sandy Forbes told her son Michael over the phone. She was trying out the words to see how they'd sound. They sounded good to her.

Not so good to Michael. "What are you talking about, Ma? You always cook a turkey at Christmas."

"Well, I'm not doing it this year." She referred to the yellow pad on which she'd done her calculations. "I've cooked fifty-five Christmas turkeys in my time. That's one a year since my mother died when I was sixteen years old. I don't want to cook one this year." The more she heard herself speak, the truer the words sounded.

Michael didn't argue. He was the youngest of her three boys, the easy-going one, and he always referred all problems to his two older brothers.

Michael hung up, and she waited, knowing the family telegraph system was as fast as it was efficient.

Easing back a little at her age wasn't a crime, she reminded herself as she prepared chocolate chip cookie dough in her old mixer in the big yellow kitchen of the big old house where she'd raised her three boys. Now she baked cookies for her seven grandchildren, who visited regularly—often for long stretches of time while their parents were busy. She'd bought the house with her husband back when they were first married and she'd lived here ever since, through marriage, three kids, widowhood. A life of ups and downs. She still cleaned the place top to bottom every week and did all her own gardening.

Five minutes later, her phone rang. She wiped her floury hands on a towel and answered the insistent ring. It was her second son, Jim. "Hey, Ma. I've got the Christmas list from the boys. They both want video games. I've made a list of titles and emailed it to you."

"Thank you, Jim." He did not, she noted, ask what was on her Christmas list. "I'm glad you called. I wanted to give you plenty of warning. I'm not cooking a turkey this year." As if Michael hadn't already told him.

"Why not?" She could almost picture his scowl. Jim liked things to stay the same.

"Because I'm a vegetarian. I don't eat turkey."

"So? You've been a veg since before I was born. You always cook the bird."

"Well, this year I'm not doing it." Couldn't they even try to understand?

"You cooked one at Thanksgiving." The memory of that meal was enough to toughen her spine.

"I know. Elspeth and Bill had a fight and then he stormed out, Brady got drunk and you threw a turkey thigh at him. The younger boys got into a fistfight and broke a lamp." Then they'd left her with all the dishes, the broken lamp, and the knowledge that on Thanksgiving not one member of her family had thought to thank her. The memory made her so mad she said, "In fact, I'm not even hosting the meal."

"What?" The sound exploded down the line. "But that's, I mean-- I gotta go. I can't even talk to you right now."

The scent of fresh-baked cookies filled the air when the phone rang yet again an hour later. "Hello, Elspeth," she said. Elspeth was her daughter-in-law. The wife of her eldest son, who was the town dentist and far too busy to be bothered by family conflict. His wife handled all that, along with everything else in his life from paying his bills to raising their three kids.

Elspeth, at least, wasn't devious. She came right to the point. "Jim says you're not hosting Christmas this year. Are you okay?"

At least someone was thinking of her. Even a little bit.

"I'm fine. I'm simply tired of always hosting every family occasion. I'm seventy-one years old. I think someone else should take a turn."

"But your house is so homey, so lived in." Elspeth's house, on the other hand, was neither of those things. She and her husband shared a compulsive neatness trait. Their designer kitchen always gleamed since they ate most of their meals out. Dust was never allowed to settle on the surfaces of their expensive furniture. Even the garden was rigidly perfect. She'd once caught her son on his hands and knees on the velvet lawn, using a pair of scissors to snip stray blades of grass the gardeners had missed. There was no possibility that her wealthy son and his wife would host Christmas dinner at their house. The mess would be intolerable.

"Thank you for saying so. But I'm not cooking the turkey dinner this year." Every time she said the words she felt a little better about them. "I'm tired."

Sandy lived in the small town of Tarlo, Washington, a city that had boomed in the early twentieth century as a logging hub. Now it limped along, losing more residents than it kept, but her family was here and it was home. Even so, she sometimes thought they were a little too close. She was beginning to realize that she'd spent a lot of years giving, giving, giving. And she loved doing it, but for some reason the disastrous Thanksgiving she'd hosted kept popping up like the Ghost of Christmas Dinner Yet to Come and she felt her body and mind rebel. No, she thought. For this one year, she was stepping down. She supposed she was waiting for someone else in the family to take on the job just this once.

Her sister dropped by the next morning with store bought donuts. Sandy put on a pot of coffee and they chatted in her kitchen for a few minutes before Karen said, "Your boys are very upset that you're letting them down for Christmas." She scolded as though the boys were helpless lads instead of grown men in their forties. Okay, they were still helpless lads but Sandy was beginning to see that it was partly her fault. "They'll be fine," she said.

Karen looked genuinely shocked. "I can't believe you're being so selfish."

"I know," Sandy said, stifling a giggle. "I can't believe it either."

"You can't ruin Christmas for the entire family. Who's going to cook the dinner?"

"What about you?"

Her sister was ten years younger, though she'd let herself go in the last few years gaining far too much weight and spending half her life at the doctor with one complaint or another. "How can you even ask that of me? You know how much my back pains me." Her sister put a hand to her back and winced. "I only wish I was strong enough to host the meal."

Sandy put up with a week of cajoling, badgering and whining. Even her eldest son, Bill the dentist, found time to call her on his cell phone on his way home from work.

"What's this I hear about Christmas?"

"I'm not hosting it this year," she said for what sounded like the hundredth time.

"What are we supposed to do?" His indignation crackled over the line, and Sandy realized at that moment that no one else was going to take on one holiday dinner. Instead they had a clear plan to browbeat her until she submitted. She didn't get mad very often, but she felt a surge of anger in that moment.

"I don't know what you're going to do, but I'm going out of town for Christmas."

She was glad he couldn't see her face. She was so shocked at the words that came out of her mouth she couldn't seem to get her jaw working fast enough to unsay them, to tell her firstborn that she was only kidding.

Amazingly, he believed her. "What about the mail?" he snapped.

Sandy ran the local post office. It was true, mail delivery was busiest at this time of year, but there were two other employees who could fill in for her and in truth she'd been thinking it might be time to retire anyway. She was as tired of selling postage stamps and shipping packages as she was of cooking turkey.

"Everyone in Tarlo will still get their mail. Don't worry."

"Go ahead, Ma. Have your holiday and leave your family in the lurch. Don't think anyone's driving you to the airport."

"Fine. I'll take a cab."

There came a point in the enterprise when it was simply too late to back out. Everyone in town knew that Sandy Forbes was going away. At Christmas! And leaving her family. There were whispers of dementia and kindly old Dr. Stevens, who was older than she was and should have retired years ago, actually called on her to have a little chat.

"How are you eating?" he asked her as he sipped tea in her living room.

"I eat well, thank you." So did he from the size of his belly. "Have another chocolate chip cookie." They were her home made ones and she was famous for them though in truth the only secret was that she put extra chocolate chips in her dough.

"Are you sleeping all right?"

"Yes," she lied. She wasn't sleeping all that well, torn between excitement at the idea of going away and guilt that she really should cook turkey number 56.

"And how's the memory?" he asked her.

"Dr. Stevens, I don't have Alzheimer's. I looked up the symptoms on the Internet. I am fine."

"Well, if you're using the Internet, your brain function is very good," he said, grinning so she'd know he was joking. "I've never been able to figure out computers." He settled back and gave her his kindly look. She used to think it was comforting, now she found it patronizing. "Sometimes, Sandy, when we get older we do irrational things that we might end up regretting."

"I'm leaving town for a week. What on earth can happen to me?"

CHAPTER 2

*W*here do you go when you've never been anywhere?

Sandy did a Google search of 'best places to spend Christmas.' The consensus of all the sites and articles that popped up was to go somewhere exotic, preferably hot and expensive. Taos, New Mexico, Florida, St. Miquel something or other in Mexico. She clicked through one spectacular locale after another. When she got to Tromslo, Norway, she gave up on Google. She wasn't looking for an exotic vacation with cabanas and drinks in coconut shells, not was she desperate to fly thousands of miles to see the Northern Lights. She didn't want to go anywhere where she needed to pack Imodium or get shots before leaving home.

All she wanted was a nice, safe place not too far from home where she could be waited on for a change. She wanted a hotel with room service and a good restaurant where a woman of a certain age eating alone on Christmas night would not raise eyebrows. There should be some nice places to walk. And, she decided, her getaway destination should not be listed on Google as a top Christmas vacation spot.

She looked at the postmarks of the mail coming through the Tarlo post office for ideas. And finally, one day, she saw it. The postmark read, Blossom Creek, Oregon. She made a sound: a sigh, a yip and a laugh all rolled uncomfortably into one choking cough that had Irv, the other postal attendant on duty, coming over to pat her on the back and ask if she was okay.

His pale blue eyes looked concerned behind the big black-framed glasses he wore ever since his wife had told him he looked like Martin Scorsese. He didn't look like the movie director. He looked like a short, homely, near-sighted postal clerk. But he had dreams of leaving Tarlo and making a new start, even though he did nothing that would get him to his goals. She had a sneaking fondness for him. "I'm fine." She showed him the envelope.

The concern she read on his face deepened. Obviously the dementia rumors had reached him. "It's a Christmas card. Lot of folks getting them this time of year."

She shook her head, impatient at how obtuse he was being. "Look at the postmark."

He pulled the envelope closer and squinted. "Blossom Creek, Oregon."

"Right. And that is where I will spend Christmas."

He pondered her words for a moment. "Probably aren't a lot of blossoms this time of year."

Maybe there wouldn't be blossoms in December in Blossom Creek, Oregon. Sandy didn't care. She looked the town up on her computer and discovered the destination fulfilled all her requirements. She could fly there in a couple of hours. There were several hotels and restaurants, parks and a good bus service.

Best of all, she would not spend the entire month of December cooking, planning, worrying and then exhausting herself on the 25th She wouldn't have to play peace keeper between siblings who should have got over sibling rivalry years ago. She wouldn't have to remember which cousins were feuding and sit them far apart, or worry that Bill's kids spent too much time on their electronic devices and were becoming antisocial, or that Karen's daughter Ashley clearly hadn't conquered the Bulimia. And, once the meal was over, she wouldn't spend the next few days cleaning up and putting away. This year she was going to be a very selfish woman.

At times she almost lost her nerve, but every time she did, she'd see in her mind her son berating his wife until she yelled back at him, at which point Bill had thrown his napkin down and stormed out. She'd see a greasy turkey thigh sailing through the air like a poultry scud missile, as her second son launched it at their drunk cousin Brady, who wasn't so drunk that he couldn't duck, so the grease and gravy soaked thigh had thwacked into her dining room curtains–requiring an expensive visit to the dry cleaners.

When her will weakened, she forced herself to do something. Book her ticket. Book a hotel. Get directions by bus from the airport in Blossom Creek to her hotel.

Sandy bought and wrapped gifts for her seven grandchildren and mailed them from the post office.

Elspeth called her a few days before she was leaving and said, "I'd love to drive you to the airport, but you know what Bill's like. If he found out he'd kill me."

"I know, dear. It's sweet of you to offer."

Elspeth took a breath. "I hope you have a wonderful time. Merry Christmas."

She worried about Elspeth, knowing her marriage wasn't ideal, but then she worried about them all. "I'll have my cell phone with me if you want to talk. Merry Christmas to you, too."

Sandy decided to drive herself to the airport and leave her car there while she was away.

When she boarded the commuter jet on December 23rd she felt absurdly excited, and a little guilty, as though she were getting away with something scandalous. A grandmother leaving her own family at Christmas time. Imagine!

When she arrived in Blossom Creek, she discovered it was quite a bit bigger a town than she'd imagined. It was really a suburb of Portland.

The sky was ominously gray and heavy and the air felt colder than at home. She huddled into her coat as she followed signs for the bus with her single rolling suitcase bouncing along behind her.

She passed a row of taxis but she felt as though she was already being ridiculously extravagant. She'd take the bus.

No sooner had the big, chugging bus pulled out of the airport and onto a highway that the snow started to fall. Big, serious flakes that meant business.

She sat up front near the bus driver who turned out to be a big, cheerful man who took her under his wing almost immediately after she asked him to make sure she got off at the right stop.

"Which stop you want?"

She consulted the directions she'd printed off the Internet. He shook his head. "This bus doesn't stop there. Where you goin'?"

"The Blossom Flower Inn." Okay, she'd booked it because the name struck her as so funny she couldn't help herself.

"Never heard of it." By this time the bus had been going for about twenty minutes. Most of the airport travelers had got off and locals were starting to get on. The driver raised his voice. "Anybody heard of The Blossom Flower Inn?"

There were murmurings and rumblings. A few passengers consulted each other. Finally, a voice from near the back of the bus yelled, "I think it's out by Wanatchee Mall."

The driver shook his head and looked at her with concern. "That's not good. This bus doesn't go anywhere near there."

Anxiety prickled her skin. She was in a strange city where she knew no one, on a bus going nowhere near where she wanted to be, afternoon was closing in to evening and the snow was falling in thick, white curtains.

What had she done?

The bus driver caught her expression and winked. "Don't worry. I ain't going to leave you stranded somewhere. A nice lady like you. Just hang on tight."

The next time the bus pulled over, the driver dug out his cell phone and placed a call. "Listen, Bud, I got a lady here who needs to go to the Blossom Flower Hotel. You know where that's at?"

While Sandy listened to the one-sided conversation hopefully, she watched the snow flakes twirl and dance outside the bus's front window.

Three vague shapes appeared at the door and the driver opened it to let them in. They were a straggly trio. Older men, each carrying a bag she suspected contained all their worldly belongings.

"Okay, here's what's going to happen," the bus driver told her after he got off the phone. "We figured out what bus you need. We're going to wait right here until your bus comes."

"Oh, but I couldn't—"

"Ma'am, there is no way I am leaving a nice lady like you to sit in the snow for a half hour."

Sandy glanced around but the few people still on the bus seemed okay with it. The three newcomers settled back to wait as though they did a lot of that.

One of them caught her eye. "I'm really sorry for any inconvenience," she said to him.

"Don't matter," he said. "The shelter won't open until nine o'clock tonight so we got some time to kill. Better in here than out there."

It was strangely pleasant on the bus, with the motor rumbling to keep the heater going and snow falling all around so she felt as though she were in the middle of a bus shaped Christmas globe and somebody had given the thing a good shake.

"You in town visiting family for the holidays?" one of the trio asked her.

"No," she said. "I'm alone."

"Not good to be alone at Christmas," another said. He looked as though he knew. Hard times radiated from his weather-beaten face.

"You should come with us to the shelter." He looked at his two companions and they both nodded. "They do a real nice dinner there. Turkey and everything. Coffee. Pie. You can sit with us and then you won't be alone."

"Thank you so much," she said, in real gratitude. "But I am going to have dinner in my hotel."

"Well, if you change your mind, you know where to find us." They chatted to her for the rest of the time she spent on the bus. They'd all experienced hardship but none of them dwelled. This was their life and they lived it as best they could.

Her three wise men turned out to be homeless men. But their gifts were as valuable as gold, frankincense and myrrh. More, probably, since she didn't even know what the last two were. They gave her acceptance, offered friendship to a stranger, and made her feel valued simply for listening to them.

After a while, a second bus pulled up behind them. "That's your ride, ma'am," her bus driver said.

"Thank you," she said. She put out her hand to the driver. "And Merry Christmas."

He shook her hand heartily. "Merry Christmas to you, too. I hope they treat you real nice at the Blossom Flower Hotel."

The second bus deposited her a block away from the hotel and she found herself in a surprisingly quiet part of town. There was a lit sign for the iHop, what looked like some kind of strip mall, and a low rise building that had to be her hotel.

She set off to trudge through about 3 inches of fresh snow, pulling her case behind her like a sled.

She hadn't planned to stay in a place so remote but she comforted herself that at least she now knew where the bus stop was.

CHAPTER 3

When Sandy entered the hotel she felt momentarily strange and shy. She didn't think she'd ever stayed in a hotel by herself before. The few times she'd paid for accommodation, she and her husband were traveling together. And once she and her sister took a bus trip through the Rockies.

Well, as her mother would have said, 'you've made your bed, girl. Now lie in it.' Only she wouldn't actually be making her bed, she thought as she approached a sign that said Reception. A wonderful blessed chambermaid would make her bed for her.

Her room in the Blossom Flower Hotel was on the third floor. She had a view of the car park, which resembled a snow sculpture of vaguely car-shaped mounds. The room was clean, the bed enormous and the bathroom was tiled in marble and stocked little bottles of shampoo and body lotion.

She unpacked her case. Then wondered what to do with herself.

It was six o'clock. She decided to go downstairs for supper.

She'd never eaten dinner alone in a hotel before. The idea seemed glamorous and cosmopolitan. She could be a traveling business woman, or someone attending some sort of conference. She had a book with her, a book club selection that June, who'd picked this month's read, had promised them wasn't depressing. She picked it up. Checked herself in the mirror before going down for dinner. Her black slacks were old but pure wool and still decent, her white blouse was neatly pressed and she wore the red and black sweater Elspeth and Bill had given her for her birthday. On impulse, she swiped some red lipstick over her mouth and tied her hair back with a black bow. She'd never dyed her hair in her life. Now it was a silver-white color and still as thick as a young woman's. If she had a vanity it was her hair. She still wore it long, hanging loose to her shoulders unless she tied it back, as she did now.

Good enough, she thought, and triple checking that she had her key card in her purse, she left the room.

When she got to the lobby, she paused. Of course, this close to the holidays there were no conferences. Probably no traveling business women, either. The only people staying here were probably in town visiting family.

The fake tree in the corner needed dusting, she thought as she passed it, then noted that the local firefighters were doing a toy drive. All the presents under the tree would be picked up tomorrow afternoon and distributed to children of less fortunate families. Of course, tomorrow was Christmas Eve. She made a mental note to purchase a gift the following day.

The Blossom Flower Inn offered both a dining room and a coffee shop. She hesitated, but quickly realized she wasn't quite brave enough to eat in the dining room by herself. Perhaps she'd have her Christmas dinner there. Instead, she headed across the lobby for the brightly lit coffee shop.

As she passed the registration desk, she heard a man say, "Where can I mail this?"

She heard the word 'mail' and she turned. After working for the postal service for thirty years, she couldn't help herself. It was like being in a store and hearing a child call, "Mom?" She still caught herself turning to the voice, even though her sons were all grown.

"There's a postal outlet in the mall over the way," the young man at the desk said.

"Thank you."

She hesitated, not wanting to interfere, but the parcel probably contained presents–which would never get where they were going in time—but probably had value.

He turned, with his parcel in hand, and she said, "Excuse me, but you need to put a return address on that package or the postal service won't take it."

He blinked at her. He was around her age, she supposed. A tall man with upright, military bearing and blue eyes that had faded with time. He wore a sports coat and gray trousers and shoes that gleamed with polish. He glanced down at the package, a frown forming.

"It's for security," she explained.

"I don't know what to put as the return address," he said, sounding a little lost. "Do I put my home address? Where I live? Or the hotel's address, where I'm staying?"

"Put your home address," she said. "Then, if the package somehow gets lost, it will come back to you."

"Thank you," he said, smiling at her as though she'd solved the national debt crisis. "I'll get a pen from the front desk."

But the young man had disappeared into the back somewhere. "I've got a pen," she said. She opened her purse and handed him the black pen she always kept clipped to her check book.

He put the parcel down on a handy table beside arm chairs that flanked a gas fireplace. He put a hand into his jacket pocket and emerged with a pair of glasses that should be in a case. He put on the glasses and carefully wrote a home address in Bend, Oregon.

The address he was sending to was local. "It's a present for my grandson," he said, handing back her pen.

"You know the package won't get to him in time." She felt she had to tell him.

"Doesn't matter. He's not there." He sounded sad. Defeated almost. "They went to Hawaii. My son and his family."

"Oh." She didn't know what else to say.

"It's my fault. They asked me to come for Christmas but I said no. Then I changed my mind. Decided to surprise them." He shook his head. "Stupid idea. You see, my wife always used to take care of things like this."

"I know." Now she understood his slightly lost expression. She thought she'd carried that around with her for at least a year after Henry died. "I didn't even know how to write a check when I lost my husband. It's silly the things we let the other person take care of."

He nodded. "Thank you again."

"You're welcome. And good luck."

He headed to the door with his package under his arm and she took her book and went to the coffee shop.

She paused on the threshold of the brightly-lit space. There were about twenty tables and a lunch counter. All the tables were empty but one which was occupied by a middle-aged couple who looked bored with each other and the food.

A waitress appeared with a fresh pot of coffee. "Seat yourself anywhere," she called out to Sandy.

She chose a table not too far from the others, thinking it would make the waitress's job easier, but not so close they'd think she was eavesdropping. Not that they were talking much.

The waitress brought her over a menu and offered her coffee which Sandy accepted. "The special tonight is lasagna," the woman said. "Vegetarian or meat." She shifted from one foot to the other as though she'd been standing too long. "It comes with salad and bread and it's nine ninety-five."

"That sounds fine," Sandy said, closing the menu. Even a quick glimpse of the rows of sandwiches and salads and pastas and rice bowls, whatever they were, had overwhelmed her. Lasagna she understood. "I'll have the vegetarian one."

She picked up her book. Started to read.

She was half way through her meal when the older gentleman she'd helped earlier paused at the entrance as she'd done. He smiled when he saw her and nodded.

She nodded back.

"Sit anywhere," the waitress told him. He took a second to make up his mind and then chose a table near Sandy's. There was snow still melting on his jacket, she noted, and his hair was damp.

"Snow's really coming down," he said to her as he settled himself.

"Did you get the parcel mailed all right?"

"Sure did. Thanks." He rubbed his hands together. They were red from the cold. She was certain his wife would have reminded him to wear gloves and a coat before heading out into a snowstorm.

The waitress came over with the pot of coffee and he accepted a cup. Then she told him about the lasagna special.

"How is it?" he asked Sandy.

"It's good."

"I'll have the meat one."

"You got it," their waitress said. And then she turned and refilled Sandy's coffee. Behind her the other couple were paying, then they left and she and her new friend were alone.

She put down her book. It hadn't held her interest anyway and said to him, "Why don't you go to Hawaii?"

CHAPTER 4

*H*e blinked at her. Put his coffee cup down. "Go to Hawaii?"

"I was thinking that if you want to see your son and grandson that maybe you should go to Hawaii."

She was appalled at her own boldness. What was she thinking? The poor man might not have any money to go to Hawaii. He could have a medical condition that prohibited him from flying. She suspected she'd lived in a small town too long where everyone knew and got involved in everyone else's business. While he seemed to ponder her words, she said, "I'm so sorry. It's none of my business."

"No. It's kind of you to take an interest. And I did think of it, but you see, I believe if they had wanted me to go with them to Hawaii, they would have invited me."

And of course he was right. His son, obviously concerned for his father on his first Christmas without his wife, had invited him. When dad refused, he was free to take the family to Hawaii. Without telling dear old pops.

"Well," she said, "He's going to feel pretty bad when he finds out you came all this way to surprise him."

His meal arrived and he thanked the waitress politely, spread his paper napkin over his lap, and shook salt and pepper vigorously over his food without even tasting it. "I don't want my son to feel bad." He took a bite of lasagna. Chewed. Swallowed. "And you know, this isn't a bad place to spend the holidays."

"I agree," she said.

By the time they'd both finished dinner, they'd shared the basics of their two lives. He was a former bank manager, retired for several years. He and his wife had had two sons, but one, a soldier, was killed in active duty. "My wife never got over Chad dying. Wasn't long after that she took sick."

"I'm so sorry."

When they'd finished dinner, he said to her, "would you like to join me by the fire for a last cup of coffee?"

She hesitated. "What about a cup of herbal tea?"

"Much better."

He called to the waitress. Made his request.

"Not a problem," she said. "You go on over. I'll bring your teas out to you."

"Thank you." He rose and politely waited for Sandy to go first.

When they were sitting opposite each other, in front of

the fire, he suddenly said, "My goodness. I don't even know your name."

"It's Sandy," she said.

"It's a pleasure to meet you, Sandy," he said. "And I'm Earl." He stood and extended his hand to her. When they shook hands, she could feel the warmth of his skin.

"Well," he said, "you know why I'm here in Blossom River. What brings you here?"

"I've run away from home," she said.

He stared at her for a startled moment, then threw back his head and laughed. He had strong teeth, she noted, clearly his own. He also had an infectious laugh, and she found herself joining in. Laughing at herself, which she probably didn't do enough of.

The server arrived with a selection of teas, two pots of hot water, slices of lemon and honey. She'd even put two cookies on a plate. Earl tried to sign the tea to the room, but she stopped him with a hand on his shoulder. "That's okay, honey. This is on the house. You two have a nice evening."

"Well, that was kind of her," he said. "Now, tell me about this running away from home business."

So she did. She told him everything, from the awful Thanksgiving dinner, one in a string of disastrous family dinners she seemed to host. "All I really wanted was for someone else to put on a meal, just once." She sighed. Sipped peppermint tea. "But instead they all tried to bully me or make me feel guilty. I got so mad I decided to run away instead. And here I am."

Earl was a good listener, she noticed. He didn't interrupt, kept his eyes on her as she spoke, and nodded in appropriate places. When she'd finished speaking, he said, "Sounds to me like they're a bunch of spoiled brats."

It was her turn to throw back her head and laugh. "Oh, dear," she said, when she could finally speak. "I shouldn't laugh, but you're right. Three grown men in their forties, a sister in her sixties, nieces and cousins galore. I've spoiled every one of them. But it's my fault, you know. I brought them up. Now I'm paying the price."

"I think," he said after pondering for a moment, "That they love you very much. Otherwise they wouldn't all turn up for every possible occasion. If they didn't love you, they'd make excuses not to come."

She hadn't really looked at things that way before.

"I suppose you're right."

"And maybe, now you've shown them you don't want to be treated like a slave, they'll smarten up."

"Do you think so?"

He shrugged. "It's Christmas. Miracles have been known to happen this time of year."

"What will you do now, for Christmas?"

"I'd like to have dinner with you, if you'd let me."

"Oh." She glanced over at him, found his cheeks slightly pinkened. "Are you asking me for a date?"

"Yes. I believe I am." He seemed stunned at the notion.

Her lips twitched. "When's the last time you asked a woman out on a date?"

"1961. No, wait, 1962. We were married in '65." His eyes

twinkled when he looked at her. "Please don't turn me down. It might take me another fifty years to work up my courage to ask a woman for dinner."

She laughed. "Earl, I'd be delighted to have Christmas dinner with you."

CHRISTMAS EVE and Wanatchee Mall was crowded with shoppers. Most looked harried, and she knew that's exactly how she'd feel if she were home. Instead, she felt relaxed. Wickedly pleased with herself. She admired the decorations, the oversized candy canes and trees and so many blinking twinkling, flashing lights that her head spun. After a while she found herself in front of a spa. They were offering a special on manicures and pedicures. Sandy had never had either.

Her nails were blunt, used to cooking, gardening and doing housework. But she didn't have to do any of those things for the next few days. And she had some time to kill.

She entered Penny's Hair and Nail Spa and asked the young girl behind the counter about an appointment. "We can take you right in," the girl said cheerfully.

An hour later, Sandy emerged sporting absurdly red nails. It was like having ten Christmas baubles on the end of her finger tips. She couldn't stop looking at them. They were so festive.

And at the other end of her she had festive feet!

Not that anyone but she would ever see them, but it was lovely to know they were there.

Across the hallway from the spa was a lingerie place, the window filled with lace and silky things that matched her nails. She longed simply to touch them. So she walked in to the store and stroked the soft silk.

"Can I help you?" a chesty red head of about forty asked her.

Sandy yanked her hand away from the rack of nighties, feeling guilty. "No. I was only looking."

"This set looks fantastic on," the much younger woman told her. "And it matches your manicure."

"I'd never wear anything like that," Sandy said, shocked the woman would even suggest such a thing. "I'm seventy-two."

The woman gazed at her for a moment. "Not to be rude, but are you recently divorced – or widowed?"

"Does twelve years count as recent?"

"Oh, honey." She ran a professional eye up and down Sandy's frame. "Size ten?"

"Usually."

She found a hangar thrust her way, the red night dress waving from it like a banner. "Try it on."

"But I'm too old," she protested.

"You're mature, not dead. Go try it on."

*S*andy's parents had grown up in the depression and she'd been taught young the value of a nickel. She and her husband had lived frugally all their lives. The most expensive thing they'd ever bought was their home, and they then worked tirelessly to pay off the mortgage. The second most expensive outlay of money had been his funeral costs. They'd helped the kids too. Helping fund their educations and buy their first homes.

She didn't make a fortune running the post office, but she didn't need a lot of money to live, either, and she faithfully saved fifteen percent of each paycheck. She owned her house and she had a tidy amount of savings.

For years she'd been buying her underwear and night things at Wal-Mart. Why shouldn't she splurge if she wanted to?

It wasn't as though anyone need ever know. She glimpsed herself in the mirror of the lingerie store. The red silk felt heavenly against her skin. Sure, it wasn't the firm, glowing skin of the models in the posters on the walls, but she walked to work every day, the house kept her busy gardening and cleaning. She ate sensibly. She looked, in fact, better than she would have imagined.

Why not? She thought.

Why the heck not?

"You okay in there?" the sales clerk called through the door.

"I'll take it," she decided, liking the happy blush on her cheeks and the gleam in her eye. "And I think I'm going to need some new underwear as well."

"You won't be sorry."

"It's a Christmas present for myself."

While she was in the mall, she also bought a Lego set, something her boys would have loved when they were young. She had it gift wrapped and trudged back through the falling snow to her hotel.

She bumped into Earl as she was placing her gift under the tree. "Hello," he said.

"Hello." She felt a tiny bit shy around him, and oddly girlish for a woman who'd been getting senior's discounts for more than seven years.

"Snow's coming down like crazy," he said, sounding a little grumpy. He held a much-folded newspaper in one hand and his reading glasses in the other.

"I know."

"My car's snowed in." He seemed to hesitate then said, "Look, I've done the Times crossword, read the paper cover to cover – even my Horoscope, so you can see I was desperate – and I've finished the book I brought with me. Would you consider going out to a movie with me tonight?"

"Because you're bored and your car's snowed in?"

"No. Because I want to take you out to the movies. And we can walk there." He sighed. Looked at her ruefully. "I really am rusty at this dating thing, aren't I?"

"Yep."

"Sandy, would you give me the pleasure of your company to the movies this evening?"

"All right then." Since she'd been thinking of watching TV in her room tonight, no doubt *Miracle on 34th Street* or *It's a Wonderful Life*, something about family that would make her nostalgic and miss her kids and grandkids, the thought going across to the theatre was a much better idea.

He seemed so pleased that she was glad she'd accepted.

They agreed to meet back in the lobby at 6 p.m. and then he said, "Well, all right then. I'd better go take a nap so I don't snore through the movie." He walked back to the elevator. She thought about going to the coffee shop for a cup of tea when the young gal at the front desk called her by name. There were so few guests staying here that she wasn't all that impressed.

"Yes?" Sandy walked to the desk.

The young woman handed her an envelope. "This came in the mail for you."

"Really?"

She took the proffered envelope and recognized Elspeth's writing. The mail had either been super efficient or Elspeth had mailed the card before Sandy even left. Either way, she was touched.

"Thank you," she said, and went to sit by the fire to open her mail. Inside, as she'd suspected, was a card. A Grandma card. And Elspeth and Bill's two boys had each written a short greeting. "Have an awesome holiday, Grandma, I'll miss you," wrote 13-year-old Benson. His ten-year-old brother had penned, "Go Wild, Grandma." She chuckled. If only they'd known, she seemed to be following both pieces of advice. Elspeth had written, "We will miss you very much, Sandy. Merry Christmas. (Please buy yourself something special from us). She'd included a hundred-dollar bill in the card.

Sandy fingered the bill. Of course, it was reckless sending cash in the mail, something she told her customers never to do, but the money had arrived. And her daughter-in-law wanted her to spend it.

Well, Sandy had already treated herself to a night dress and new underwear, which felt wonderful on. But she had a date for Christmas dinner, and an order to buy herself something.

When was the last time she'd bought a new dress?

Or had a date?

Knowing the stores would soon be closing, she put her coat on one more time and stomped back out into the snow. She'd come to love the feeling of stepping out into a true winter wonderland. Since she didn't have to drive anywhere or shovel the drive or worry about getting groceries, she could simply enjoy the feeling of stepping into a Christmas card.

The mall was now fairly thin of shoppers. A few harried looking men dashed down the mall aisles looking desperate, but otherwise it was calm. Storekeepers were clearly watching their clocks waiting to go home.

She'd seen the dress in the window of a women's dress shop and paused earlier in the day. Knowing how much money she'd already spent on self-indulgent foolishness she hadn't even stepped inside. But Elspeth's gift was a sign. She walked in and the bored-looking clerk brightened up. "Can I help you?"

"Yes. Would you have that blue dress in the window in a size ten?"

"I think so. And we're already starting our Boxing Day Sale," she said. "It's twenty percent off."

Even at twenty percent off Sandy spent a little more than the hundred dollars, but she didn't care. The dress brought out the blue in her eyes and looked elegant and stylish.

She'd wear her sensible black pumps with the low heel on her Christmas date. Date! She couldn't believe how excited she felt. She was like a girl again.

"I'll take it."

"It looks beautiful on you," the clerk said. "I hope you're not cooking dinner in that dress."

"No. I'm being taken to dinner by a gentleman."

"Wow. You're so lucky. Me, I'm cooking dinner for a

seventeen, including my mother-in-law who only shows up so she can criticize every single thing I do. I wish I could tell her where to stick the turkey."

"I know. I've been thinking that maybe people treat us that way because we've let them for so long. I'm beginning to believe that if you change, they'll have to adapt too. It's not easy, but why don't you try telling your mother in law that if her way with mashed potatoes is so much better you'd love to come to her for dinner next year."

The overtired clerk began to laugh. "Can you imagine the look on her face?" She rang up the purchase. "Maybe I will."

"Happy Holidays."

"Same to you."

Sandy made one more purchase on her way out of the mall. She bought Earl a case for his glasses and had it gift-wrapped.

Sandy and Earl didn't end up going to the movies after all.

When they checked the local paper and reviewed the movies playing at the theater across the street, there were two action films, two animated movies for children and a horror movie.

"I'd take you downtown for dinner but—"

"No, no. I wouldn't want you driving in this."

"Well—" he seemed completely at a loss.

"You know," she said, "There are pay-per-view movies in our rooms, and I'm sure the old standbys from when we were kids will be on regular TV."

"You'd trust me in your room?"

"Yes, I believe I would."

"I promise to behave like a perfect gentleman." He brightened up. "And we could order room service."

And that's what they did. They ordered cheese pizza and salad and soft drinks from the room service menu and watched *It's a Wonderful Life* on TV. She didn't feel sad or nostalgic. She knew her kids would be fine without her and she, Sandy Dremen, was seventy-two years old and entertaining a single man in her bedroom. And they were having fun. Talking and laughing until past midnight when he reluctantly put his shoes back on and said, "I'd better go now or I'll ruin your reputation."

She rolled herself off the bed and stood. "That was much more fun than watching television alone on Christmas Eve."

"I can't even tell you how nice it was for me," he said. "I look forward to our date tomorrow."

"Me, too."

He looked at her for a moment as though he might kiss her, then instead, reached out and patted her shoulder.

"Good night."

*S*andy woke the next morning as excited about Christmas day as she'd been when she was a child.

Huge, white snowflakes drifted lazily down. She wondered idly if she'd be able to fly out on the 27th as planned and realized she didn't really care.

She called her family, every one of them, and wished them a Merry Christmas. Her kids were all doing their own things this year without her to pull the group together, but everyone sounded reasonably happy. Bill and his family would be eating in a fancy restaurant, her other boys were having dinner at home with their families and her sister Karen had managed to get herself and her family invited to a cousin's.

She shook her head as she finished her last call. She'd stepped down from the role of Super Grandma and nothing terrible had happened.

Today was for her. She dressed warmly, ate a quick breakfast in the coffee shop and then went for a long walk. There was a path that wound through the streets behind the hotel and with her sturdy boots on she could navigate the winding trail fine. She felt as though she had the world to herself, but after a while she heard carol singing and saw she was near a church. She followed the sound of song and slipped into the back of the church, not caring what denomination it was.

The pews were full but a nice young family scrunched over and made room for her. As she sat and listened to the service, glanced around at all the people with their different stories and lives coming together, she felt a deep sense of gratitude. She was old enough to have seven grandchildren and still young and healthy enough to have an adventure. Her life might be heading into its winter, but winter was a glorious season.

Sandy walked back to the hotel and headed to her room to bathe and primp. She had, after all, a date.

WHEN SHE ENTERED the lobby in her new blue dress, her makeup and hair freshly done, her manicure and pedicure still perfect and her lovely new underwear making her feel like a much younger, vital woman, she found Earl waiting for her. He wore a suit. She was thrilled to find he'd bothered with his appearance, too.

His face lit up when he saw her. "Sandy, you look beautiful," he said.

"Thank you."

Christmas carols filled the air from the hotel sound system and there was a happy energy in the lobby. A few family groups stood at the entrance to the dining room waiting to be seated.

"Ready for dinner?"

"Yes."

It was six o'clock, but they'd discovered they both disliked eating late. They headed for the hotel dining room.

While they waited behind the families ahead of them, Sandy perused the room. It was fairly full of couples, families, a few singles. A menu affixed to the wall told her that this was a pre-set meal. Turkey and all the trimmings.

Why had she never thought to check? She's simply assumed there would be a full menu of choices.

Well, she thought, it will be like every other Christmas. She'd eat mashed potatoes and vegetables and try to ignore the smell of turkey.

Then she glanced at Earl and saw that he looked stricken.

She followed his gaze and realized he was looking at all the family groups and the couples and experiencing one of those piercing moments of grief that she remembered well.

She made a decision. She hoped it was the right one.

Turned, pasted a panicked expression on her face and said, "Earl, I'm a vegetarian."

"You are?"

"Yes. I thought there'd be a full menu." She shrugged helplessly, stepping away from the line. "I can't eat a turkey dinner."

She watched the stricken look fade from his face as he stepped into his new role of problem solver. He turned his back on the busy restaurant. In relief, she was certain.

Put his hands in his pockets and rocked on his heels. "Well, I don't think the coffee shop is even open."

She was about to tell him she'd changed her mind, that she'd eat the vegetables, when she had an idea. "You know what I'd really like?" she said.

"What?"

"Pancakes."

"Pancakes?"

"Why not? There's an iHop right across the street."

"You want to go to the International House of Pancakes for Christmas dinner?" She began to realize he wasn't as flexible in his thinking as she was.

She touched his arm. "Earl, maybe we both need to get away from some memories this year."

He blinked rapidly, then nodded. "Pancakes. What a fine idea. We'd better get our coats and boots."

A few minutes later they met once more in the lobby, both bundled up for winter. He held out his arm. She put her gloved hand in the crook and they headed out into the snow.

The iHop wasn't doing a roaring business, but it was open and there were other diners there.

Perhaps they were a little overdressed for their

surroundings, but Sandy didn't care. Now that they'd left the families and the turkeyfest behind, Earl had brightened up and she was experiencing the joy of doing something unexpected and a little foolish.

She loved every minute of it.

"I am going to have a large order of blueberry pancakes." She leaned forward and added, "With syrup *and* butter *and* whipped cream."

He put his glasses on and scanned the menu. "Do you mind if I have sausages with mine?"

"Of course not."

Once they'd placed their orders and had coffees in front of them, he took off his glasses and placed them on the table, then reached into his pocket looking a little self-conscious and pulled out a small wrapped Christmas present which he put in front of her.

"Oh, Earl."

She opened the package and discovered a Rudolph the red-nosed reindeer lapel pin. When you pushed a button, the nose lit up. She was delighted with it.

She lit up the nose and carefully affixed the pin to her new dress.

She dug into her purse and handed him his gift. His cheeks pinkened. "You got me a gift."

When he unwrapped the glasses case, he glanced up in amazement, as though she might be psychic. "How did you know I lost my case?"

"Because you keep sticking your glasses in your pocket, unprotected."

"Well," he said, shaking his head. "Well."

He slipped the glasses in his case. "A perfect fit."

Once dinner was over, they walked back to the hotel. The snow had stopped falling and the world was quiet and still.

He stopped her before they entered the hotel. "The best gift I've had was meeting you," he said, and leaned forward to kiss her.

She touched his cheek.

They pulled away and walked into the hotel.

The dining room was thinning out, but the carols still played, and the festive mood lingered. "Could I interest you in a night cap?" he asked.

"Yes. I believe you could." They sat at a tiny table for two and he had a brandy while she ordered a glass of red wine. When she lifted her wine, the glow of Rudolph's nose was reflected in the glass.

He reached for her hand. "Sandy, I know we've only known each other for a couple of days, but I want to know you better." He took a breath. "Would you come home with me, to Bend? I've got a nice house and I'd like to show you where I live, and introduce you to my friends. I—I'm seventy-four years old and I feel like I'm falling in love again."

She let her hand rest in his. There was a pianist in here, playing White Christmas on a grand piano. She let the music swirl around her. Sipped her wine.

Then she said, "No."

She squeezed his hand. "Earl, your wife's only been

gone six months. You haven't finished grieving yet. I don't want to be the woman you jumped at because she was the first woman you met and we were snowed in and it was magical."

"But—I thought you felt the same."

She smiled, a tiny, happy secret smile. "I do. But I'm not a foolish young woman, and I certainly don't plan to be a foolish old one. I am going to get on a plane tomorrow and go home. I miss my crazy family. And you're going to go home, to your house and your friends."

He nodded, sadly.

"And, if you still want to see me, let's say a month or two from now, let's meet up in Hawaii."

"Hawaii?"

"Yes. I've never been. We'll get some sun, get to know each other. And scandalize our families. Your son can go there without inviting you. I say we go and don't invite any of them."

"Hawaii," he said again.

Then she had a qualm. "Did you and your wife ever go to Hawaii?"

"No. She disliked hot places."

"Then it's perfect. No memories. Until we make some of our own."

He sat for a moment, idly playing with her hand. Then he said, "All right. It's a date."

They sat and listened to the music and talked, while they held hands and possibilities shimmered.

As the evening grew longer, Sandy realized that her one selfish act of standing up for herself really hadn't turned out that badly.

In fact, running away for the holidays was the best Christmas present Sandy could have imagined.

GRANDMA CATCHES A WAVE

CHAPTER 1

"*Happy New Year. I miss you.*"

Sandy Forbes read the words on the greeting card one more time, even though she'd nearly worn through the card stock opening and closing the thing, and she'd long ago memorized the words.

She enjoyed looking at Earl's neat handwriting. It had been such a long time since a man had romanced her that she'd forgotten the thrill of being wanted. She touched the front of the card. It was fairly standard Happy New Year fare—a champagne bottle popping, balloons flying and sparkles winking, but it meant that Earl had been thinking of her. He had gone to a card store and chosen this one. She could picture him, tall, conservatively dressed and no doubt removing his glasses from the case she had bought him for Christmas so he could see the cards properly.

To a woman who had been the postmistress of the small town of Tarlo, Washington for many years now, handling mail and packages all day long, it was wonderful to receive this piece of mail all for her.

She and Earl had met only a few weeks ago when she had run away from home to spend Christmas on her own. How could she have known that she would end up eating her Christmas dinner in a pancake restaurant and that she would find romance at seventy-one years old.

Happy New Year.

What did that even mean?

For many years she'd crafted a list of New Year's resolutions. Each year's were sadly similar to the ones from the year before. Her list included things like lose weight, learn Spanish, try to be more tolerant.

This year, however, she felt that if she wrote a list of resolutions she might actually do the things on it. Sandy liked lists, she liked to see her neat handwriting on yellow lined paper. She enjoyed ticking off items as she accomplished them. She put the card back on the mantelpiece where it held pride of place in the center, among her family photographs. There was her late husband, the man she'd been married to for more than forty years. There were her three boys, all with their own wives and families now.

After her husband died, she had simply carried on. She had worked through her grief, thankful to have her job at the post office to keep her mind off her pain. She'd accepted her role as widowed grandmother and continued to host all the holidays and family birthdays. She'd even loved babysitting her grandkids.

But now, who needed her? Her grandkids were all in school and had their own busy lives. Her boys, though she knew they loved her, treated her as some combination of a cash machine, an unpaid servant and a mild embarrassment.

She couldn't resist. She opened the New Year's card once more. There wasn't only a message inside. There was also a ticket to Hawaii.

Hawaii! Sandy had never been off the continental United States. For goodness sake, she'd barely been outside Washington State. And here she was contemplating flyting to a tropical paradise at the invitation of a recently widowed man she had only known a few weeks.

Would she go? Should she go?

There was no one to ask. She glanced around and felt the emptiness in the rooms of the house she'd lived in for half a century. The old craftsman was far too big for one person. It smelled of lemon wax because she cleaned the house herself, religiously, every week. The labor was making her back ache. The rain fell outside her window, painting everything soggy and gray. Unlike Hawaii where she imagined the sun always shone.

She would make a list. Lists were very good for helping clarify her thoughts.

She picked up a blue ballpoint pen, found a partially used pad of yellow foolscap and wrote at the top of a clean page: *New Year's Resolutions*. She underlined her headline.

She wrote the number 1. Beside it, she wrote: *Retire from the Post Office*.

She looked down at the pad and gazed at those words as though someone else had penned them. Retire from the post office? When had she decided to retire? Truth was, she'd been thinking on and off for a few years now that it was time. She didn't need to work. She had savings, a small pension, and, of course, the house, which she owned free and clear.

Naturally, everyone in town, including Sandy herself, had assumed she would continue in her position until they found her dead one day among the mislabeled packages that had never been delivered.

But she could retire. She could be free. Free to travel to places like Hawaii.

Back to the list. She stared at those words and excitement began to build. Hawaii.

Number 2: *Go to Hawaii.*

Immediately, she pictured white sand beaches, warm turquoise waters, grass skirts and leis, the pungent smell of tropical flowers. Imagined herself in the scene she'd created. Which led immediately to:

Number 3: *buy a new bathing suit.*

The last bathing suit Sandy had owned had been black and about as flattering as a nun's habit. Perfect to take the grandkids to the outdoor pool in the summertime. She also used to swim lengths at the indoor pool in the recreation center, but, somewhere along the line, she'd lost the habit. She used to love swimming. She had been on the swim team back in her high school days. Maybe it was time to buy herself a new bathing suit.

Number 4:

Sandy left number four blank. Plenty of ideas sprang to her mind, but she felt the three items already on her list were about all she could handle at the moment.

She calculated the time, picked up the phone and called Earl. Sandy had embraced the computer age. She liked shopping online, she enjoyed emailing and she even paid bills and conducted most of her banking through the Internet.

Earl, however, was not so forward thinking. He'd come of age in the era of secretaries and dictation. He owned a computer but claimed he couldn't type and avoided email. So, they talked on the phone. Which was fine. She liked the sound of his voice and when they spoke she felt connected to him.

She heard his phone ring. He had told her that he lived in Bend, Oregon, but she'd never seen so much as a picture of his house so it was hard to imagine where he was at this moment. He answered, as he always did, "hello?"

And, as she always did, she said, "hello, Earl. This is Sandy." One day, she would introduce him to the benefits of call display.

"Sandy!" His voice was so full of surprised delight that she immediately rethought the idea of call display. She enjoyed hearing his surprise when he knew it was her on the other end of the phone.

"I just received your New Year's card."

"I hope you didn't think it was a strange thing to receive a happy New Year's card in the middle of January."

"Not at all. It was Christmas when I met you. We were barely even home by the 31st."

"Exactly." He didn't mention the ticket but she could hear him silently wondering.

"I cannot believe you sent me a ticket to Hawaii."

"I almost can't believe I did either," he admitted. "But after you suggested that we meet again in Hawaii I couldn't get the idea out of my head. There's no obligation of course. I made certain that you could cash in the ticket and use it for something else."

"Earl, I cannot imagine anything I would rather do than go to Hawaii with you." Now that she'd said it, she'd committed to going. She felt like a young girl again, fluttery and thrilled and a little uncertain.

"I am so happy you said yes. I wasn't sure if I was being too forward. The truth is, I'm rusty at all this stuff."

"Well, that makes two of us."

"Now, the ticket's open so we should decide when we want to go. I've cleared my schedule." He chuckled. "Actually, my schedule's pretty much empty. I'm looking at the calendar on my kitchen wall and the only things on it are appointments with my dentist and my financial advisor."

"I'd like a little time to tidy things up here." She took a deep breath and then glanced at her neatly penned list. "I have decided to retire from the post office." Saying the words aloud made them seem much more real.

"That's fantastic news," he said sounding genuinely excited. "You won't believe the freedom retirement gives you. We'll be able to travel more and maybe you could come down here and spend some time with me, see if you like Bend." He paused and then said, "but I'm getting ahead of myself."

She was thrilled that he was thinking of her as part of his life but she was also a naturally cautious woman and he was much more recently widowed than she was. "Let's see how we get on in Hawaii."

"Of course, yes. Do you have a preference for which island we go to?"

"Earl, I've never been to Hawaii. I've never really been anywhere."

"I took the liberty of visiting my travel agent and she found us a very nice resort on the water in Maui. I've booked us adjoining rooms for the first two weeks of February. But, of course, it's very easy to change if you'd rather go somewhere else, or that time doesn't suit you."

She liked the delicacy with which he mentioned that he'd booked them separate rooms. She also liked that he was a man who could organize things, even without the Internet. "I think that sounds wonderful. I can tell them at work that I'm retiring. I'll be giving my two weeks' notice."

"Will they be able to replace you in time?"

She grinned, even though he couldn't see her. "I guess they'll have to."

CHAPTER 2

"*A*re you out of your mind?" Her eldest son stared at her in utter disbelief. He was the most financially successful of her children, and either that, or his nature, made him think he knew better than anybody else.

"No. I do not believe I am out of my mind." She held a pleasant smile on her face and refused to get angry simply because Bill was.

"You can't just get on a plane and head off to some deserted island with a man you barely know. What about your reputation?"

Was she really going to be labeled as some wild-living scarlet woman because she was taking a holiday with a man who was not her husband? She thought about the gossips in Tarlo and decided that yes, she would be gossip fodder for weeks. However, as she was perfectly aware, it wasn't *her* reputation he was worried about. "Maui is hardly a deserted island."

He ignored her as though she hadn't even spoken. Bill had dropped by her house on his way home from his dental practice. He didn't accept her invitation to sit down. He didn't even take his coat off. What he did do was pace. It was like watching a tennis match, her eyes going left then right then left and right as he tracked back and forth across the old rug in the living room. "And you're quitting your job?"

"I am going to be seventy-two years old this year. I think I've earned the right to retire, don't you?"

Bill turned to her, and she thought it was a shame that his good looks were being ruined by the grooves of discontent marring his face. "And don't think I'm supporting you in your old age."

"I don't recall asking you to." She'd had a conversation with the bank manager, whom she'd known for years. He was probably the closest thing Tarlo had to a financial planner and, after running the numbers through a computer program, he assured her she was in good shape. "Dennis at the bank says I'll be just fine. And, if I run through my pension and savings, I'll always have the house to fall back on."

He glared at her once more. She suspected that, in spite of his wealth, he counted her assets as partly his own since he'd inherit one day. "I hope your boy toy doesn't steal it all."

She was so stunned her jaw dropped open. "My boy toy? Earl is older than I am."

"I don't care how old he is. You're a lonely old widow

who's barely ever been outside this town. You're an easy target for a con man."

She tried not to let her hurt show, but his words stung. "Do you really think I'm that naïve?"

He must've heard the edge of anger in her clipped tone, for he changed tack. "Look, ma, you've got a good life here. A decent home, family, why would you want to leave it to go running off with some stranger?"

"I'm glad you mentioned the advantage of having family nearby. I can't, for the life of me, change the light bulb in the hall. It's too high for me to reach, and I'd be frightened to fall off a ladder. Could you fetch the big ladder from downstairs and change the bulb for me while you're here?"

Bill looked at her as though she'd asked him to clean out her septic tank with his bare hands. "Stopping here has made me late for dinner as it is. I've got to go, but think about what I said." As he walked out the front door he said, "and get somebody to shovel this front walk. I nearly slipped on the way to your front door."

And who exactly did he think was going to shovel her front walk?

BILL'S WIFE, Elspeth, stopped by the next day as Sandy was baking. The smell of gingersnaps filled the kitchen. "Put on the kettle, you're just in time. The first batch of cookies is coming out of the oven."

Elspeth breathed in appreciatively. "Your house always smells so good, like fresh baking and lemon furniture polish." She put the kettle on to boil and then sat at Sandy's kitchen table. Elspeth took her job as the town dentist's wife as seriously as her son took his job as the only dentist. Her hair was freshly done, her clothes more stylish than anyone else's in Tarlo.

Sandy slipped her hands into oven mitts and pulled the tray of gingersnaps from the oven and clattered it to the stovetop. Her cooling racks were so old she thought they had belonged to her own mother. Her old mixer was a relic. A wedding present. Even her recipe was old; she'd been making the same ginger cookies for more than fifty years.

She and Elspeth chatted easily as she transferred the hot cookies to the cooling rack and put the next batch in the oven. By that time, the kettle was boiling and she made tea. They talked about Elspeth and Bill's children, how they were doing at school, the latest science experiment that had gone horribly wrong.

Sandy knew that Elspeth had not come here to talk about science experiments and school projects. She waited until they were sitting at the round table in the big, yellow kitchen where her own children had worked on their homework and their science projects. She poured tea and set out a plate of the fresh-baked cookies.

"I shouldn't, but I can never resist." Elspeth took a cookie and bit in, moaning in exaggerated pleasure. "No one bakes like you. I always tell the children how lucky they are to have a grandmother living close. I never did, you know."

Before Elspeth got too carried away sharing the tragedy of her miserable grand-parentless childhood, Sandy said, "I had a visit from your husband yesterday."

Elspeth didn't pretend to be surprised. She put her half eaten cookie on the saucer of the teacup pattered with faded roses. "I know. He mentioned it. He's very upset."

"He's my son and I love him, but that man spends far too much of his time upset. It's not good for him."

Elspeth nodded. They'd talked about Bill's bad temper before, but she was still a loyal wife. "He worries about you."

"That's nice of him, but he doesn't need to. I am seventy-one years old. I'm old enough to take care of myself."

"He's worried that you're going to be taken advantage of."

Sandy rose from her chair and walked to the fireplace. She reached for the Happy New Year card, touched it lovingly before she handed it to her daughter-in-law. "Take a look at that."

Elspeth opened the card and Sandy watched her eyes open wide as she took in the plane ticket. She read the message and then glanced up. "He's really serious, isn't he?"

"I think what you forget when you're young is that time starts to run out. We are already in our seventies. We both lost our partners. How much time do you think we have?"

"But this is so sudden." Elspeth read the card again.

"I know. It is. And maybe, after two weeks in Hawaii we'll realize that we're both happier by ourselves, in our separate cities. But maybe we'll find that life is a little more special when we're together then it is when we're apart."

Elspeth rose and replaced the card on the mantelpiece. "Honestly, I don't know what I'd do without you. We don't want you to leave."

Sandy was rather touched. "It's two weeks in Hawaii, in separate rooms, but you have to promise not to tell your husband that. He hasn't asked me to marry him."

"But what if he does? What will you do?"

It wasn't that Sandy hadn't contemplated what the future might be like with Earl. Of course she had. But she was also sensible enough to realize that they really didn't know each other all that well and at the end of two weeks they might decide simply to be friends. "Even if we did, we might decide to live here, or in his town, or perhaps we'd start somewhere that was fresh for both of us. We'd never be more than a few hours away by car. An hour by plane."

"I don't want to lose you. You're not only my mother-in-law, you're one of my best friends."

Sandy reached over and touched her hand. "Then I hope you will want me to be happy."

"I do." There was a tiny smile playing around her lips. "And I know a great store that sells bathing suits."

At that moment, Sandy realized her list of New Year's goals was still sitting in the middle of the kitchen table. She glanced up at her daughter-in-law, "you do?"

"Yep. And it's a Saturday afternoon. Bill took the boys to their hockey lessons. I'm free until six o'clock."

The timer went off and Sandy took the rest of the cookies out of the oven, packed some in a tin to send home with Elspeth and then she freshened her lipstick, grabbed her purse and her coat, slipped into her boots and they headed off.

Elspeth drove, in her-almost new silver SUV, for almost an hour before they hit a shopping mall that Sandy rarely visited. They parked and Elspeth led the way inside. January sales signs were everywhere and bargain hunters packed the aisles.

"Here we are," Elspeth said, gesturing to the store front.

Sandy was shocked. "This place sells nothing but bathing suits."

"I know. There's a great selection, too. We will find you something that will make Earl's eyes pop out of his head. He'll be proposing before you get your first sunburn."

She was glad that her daughter-in-law had clearly decided that this holiday was a good thing for Sandy. At least she had one ally. She had a feeling she was going to need all the support she could get.

CHAPTER 3

*S*andy and Earl met in Seattle at SeaTac airport. Sandy hadn't seen him in more than a month and she wondered if her imagination had built him into something he wasn't.

But, when she spotted him, looking around, obviously searching for her, she felt her heart turn over. He was already dear to her.

He appeared slightly anxious, as though he were afraid she wouldn't show up. He dragged a roll-on bag behind him and in his hand was a single yellow rose. She could tell immediately it wasn't from a florist. She walked towards him and, since she'd seen him before he'd seen her, she had the pleasure of watching his face light up when he first caught sight of her.

"Sandy." He stopped a foot away from her and simply looked at her as though drinking in her face. She suspected she was doing the same thing. "I am so happy to see you." He leaned forward and kissed her briefly. Already his scent was familiar. His aftershave was pleasant and light. It didn't smell like the modern scents her sons wore, either. She suspected Earl had been wearing the same aftershave since he first began shaving.

He handed her the single rose. It was wrapped in damp paper towel and tin foil. The delicate yellow petals were barely unfurled.

"Oh, how beautiful." She couldn't imagine where he'd found such a thing at this time of year.

"There's a sunny spot on my back patio and this old rose sometimes throws out a bloom when you least expect it. It seemed like a miracle." He grinned at her. "No, it seemed like a sign."

She leaned forward, putting her nose to the bloom, catching the light fragrance.

"It was a silly thing to bring. You won't be able to take it on the plane with you."

"No. It's perfect. I'm so glad you did."

That's when she knew he'd been as nervous about this trip as she was. But now that she was here, she didn't feel nervous anymore. She reached into the bag hanging over her shoulder, the one she'd brought for the plane, and pulled out the cellophane bag. "I brought you something from my home, too. I brought you a selection of my home-made cookies."

He opened the bag immediately and peered inside. "You don't know how much I have missed home-baked cookies." He grinned like a little kid. "Are those peanut butter? Peanut butter are my favorite."

"Yep. Peanut butter, chocolate chip, and gingersnaps." She'd put four of each kind in a sandwich bag and then placed them all in a larger freezer bag.

"We both brought something special from our own lives." She thought perhaps that was a sign, too.

Flights arrived and left, neon boards constantly updated, people hugged good-bye and hello. She felt as though a million stories were being acted out before her eyes. One woman, about her own age, turned from seeing her family off. Sandy felt her sadness as though it were her own. She stepped forward and offered the woman her rose. "Here," she said. "I can't take this on the plane. Would you like it?"

The woman's sadness lifted as she accepted the flower. "The last time anyone gave me flowers my husband was still alive. Thank you."

Sandy had never been a jet setter. She could count on one hand the number of times she'd even flown, so when they boarded their flight for Hawaii, she felt a rush of excitement. Here she was, a respectable grandmother, the kind who baked cookies, and she was flying to a tropical paradise with a man she'd only met six weeks ago. She felt ridiculously proud of herself.

"What are you grinning about?" He asked as they settled into their seats side-by-side.

"My life has always been so predictable. I don't want you to think I'm complaining. It hasn't been a bad life. In fact, it's been a pretty good one. But you get to a certain point and you look ahead and you see the whole path laid out ahead of you, right up until the end. But somehow I took a sharp right turn and now I'm on a whole new path.

He chuckled softly. "I guess it was the same for me. After my wife passed, I could see that my life would be Rotary Club meetings, seeing my son and his family when they had time. Puttering around my house and garden until I got too old to keep them up." He reached out and took her hand. As the plane lifted off he said, "I don't know where we're going but I like that the direction is up."

"Do you feel that?" she asked.

"Feel what?"

She drew in a deep breath as she lifted her face to the sunshine. "The warm, balmy air. I've heard about tropical breezes, but I've never experienced them before."

He grinned at her. "Wait till you put your feet in the water. Then you'll know you're in Hawaii."

She gawked like the tourist she was as the cab drove them along the island and she was treated to view after stunning view of blue, sparkling ocean and white sand beaches.

The resort was near a place called Kaanapali. She liked it right away. It appeared comfortable, stylish without being snobby. Set back from the beach, with white buildings scattered amongst tropical gardens, it was the kind of place where she could imagine relaxing for two glorious weeks.

They checked in and a smiling Polynesian woman give them a warm welcome along with their key cards and directed them to their rooms. A path wound through a garden, lush with tall dark green vines she didn't recognize, palm trees and flowers that she'd only ever seen in a florist's shop. Hibiscus, Bougainvillea and the waxy red blooms of Anthurium.

When they reached the doors that led to their rooms he said, "What would you like to do first?" Then, added, "perhaps you'd like to rest, maybe take a nap after that long flight."

"I want to put my feet in that ocean. Let's get our bathing suits on and I'll race you to the beach."

He laughed in delight. "You're on."

She was giggling as she pushed open the door into her room. It was a lovely room, with a comfortable queen size bed, a desk with a phone on it, a television and a small kitchenette. A connecting door must lead to Earl's room.

She didn't even stop to unpack. She scrambled into her bathing suit, so happy that her daughter-in-law had helped her choose it. The suit was a one piece that, while it offered lots of coverage, was also stylish and the blue color, according to her daughter-in-law, was perfect with her eyes, her skin tones, and her silver white hair.

At Elspeth's insistence, she'd also bought matching flip-flops and a pretty blue and white beach cover-up. She might be about to throw herself in the ocean, but she was still practically on a first date, so she took the extra time to brush her teeth and freshen her makeup.

When she stepped outside her room, carrying the beach bag that her daughter-in-law had pressed on her as a gift, Earl was standing outside.

He clearly didn't have a daughter-in-law who would take him bathing suit shopping. His trunks were faded with age. She suspected they'd started life Navy blue but years, sun and chlorine had faded them to the color of an old fishing boat. She imagined he'd had those flip-flops since he was a boy. He had no cover-up. He draped a towel around his neck, but she could see his upper body while a little on the thin side was still surprisingly muscular.

They giggled like children as they ran to the water's edge. They lay out their towels on the warm sand and then, refusing to feel too self-conscious, she shucked her cover up. Even though she walked every day, and her household chores certainly kept her physically active, her body had carried her around for seven decades. She'd borne three children. Her skin would never be dewy again and a couple of varicose veins streaked her legs with blue.

She stepped out of her flip-flops, happy that she'd treated herself to a manicure and pedicure before her holiday. She'd chosen her nail color for its name: Tropical Sunset.

She ran into the water and forgot all about her varicose veins and her aging skin as the warm water splashed over her. "This is wonderful."

Earl seemed to be enjoying her first experience in the

Hawaiian waters as much as she was. "Can you swim?" he asked.

"Can I swim?" She pointed to her chest. "Swim team captain in high school."

Then, to prove she hadn't forgotten how, she dove into a wave and stroked strongly out into the deeper water. The waves were was so warm, so buoyant, she felt as though she could float here forever. She flipped onto her back, blinking against the sun that was sliding lower toward the horizon as afternoon advanced.

Earl kept up fine. He was clearly a swimmer too. They stayed out for ages swimming, floating, then, when she felt the fatigue in her muscles, they headed back in.

As they collapsed onto their towels, he said, "I haven't had that much fun in years."

She settled back, digging her heels into the soft sand, closing her eyes and enjoying the warmth. "Well, get used to it. We are going to enjoy every minute of this vacation."

He was silent for a minute and then he said, "You know, that's a gift you have. The ability to take pleasure in everything."

She smiled sleepily. "How do you know that about me?"

"I saw it in Blossom Creek, Oregon. At Christmas. You made blueberry pancakes for Christmas dinner seem like a huge adventure."

She laughed. "It was an adventure."

"It was." He reached out and took her hand. "Thank you."

His hand was warm curled around hers. She didn't have to ask what he was thanking her for. She knew. He'd been so lost, his first Christmas as a widower. And instead of heartache and tears, she'd given him pancakes for Christmas dinner.

"Once you get past the first, it gets easier," she assured him. "The first Christmas, first time the calendar reminds you it's their birthday, the anniversary of their death, those days will always be hard. But with each year, it will get better." She turned to squint at him. "I promise."

He turned his head and met her gaze, suddenly serious. "Do you think I'm using you to get over her?"

Her voice was soft with compassion. "Of course, you are. And I am happy to help you do that." She squeezed his hand. "But I think there's something else going on here, too, don't you?"

He returned the pressure of her hand. "Yes, I do. And thank you for understanding. Now I don't feel so guilty."

"You have nothing to feel guilty about." She turned over on her stomach. Even though she was wearing sunscreen, she couldn't undo the habits of a lifetime of turning her body in the sun, like a roast on the spit, so as to brown evenly.

After a while he said, "we should probably clean up for dinner."

"Dinner?"

"My travel agent gave me a list of restaurants she recommends in the area. I thought we might try one tonight." He looked a little sheepish. "In fact, I took the liberty of reserving at a place called the Hula Grill. My travel agent said it was great. And I thought you'd like the name."

Sandy would never regret her marriage. She'd been happy and they'd worked hard together, raised their boys, experienced the ups and downs of a life shared. But she couldn't help but compare the man she'd been married to with the man who could organize a dinner reservation from five hundred miles away. She'd always been the one to organize everything from family vacations to their social calendar. She loved that Earl was an organizer and that he'd known she'd want to eat in a place called the Hula Grill. "Wonderful."

CHAPTER 4

*W*hen they were seated in the restaurant, enjoying views that she could never tire of, they perused the menu.

"Have you ever had mahi-mahi?" Earl asked.

"Mahi-mahi? I don't know if that's a massage technique or a South Asian language."

His eyes crinkled when he was amused. "It's a fish." He whispered the words as though she might be a hick who'd never traveled anywhere in her life.

"Is it tasty?"

"I hear it is. But I'm sure the steak is fine too." Then a look of horror crossed his face. "You still a vegetarian?"

"I am."

After much discussion, he had the mahi-mahi and she ordered the localicious salad. He ordered wine like a man who knows what he's doing and then they chatted, about everything and nothing. She was so happy she worried she'd wake up in her own bed and discover she'd invented everything from Earl to her new bathing suit. "You know where we go to eat in Tarlo?"

"Where?"

"It could make you dizzy choosing between all the different dining choices. There's The Lumberjack Bar and Grill, though it's more bar than grill, and Tiny's."

"Tiny's?"

She nodded. "Yep. It's an in-joke. Tiny is probably the biggest man in Tarlo. He runs a diner attached to the garage, also called Tiny's."

He waited but she was done.

"That's it?"

"That's it."

"You are starved for culture and good food."

"Yes, I am." Also, for this. The company of an interesting man her own age.

He shook his head. "Good thing I have a list from the travel agent. We'll try all of the restaurants she suggested."

She was not inclined to argue, though she suspected they'd both run out of steam and be only too happy to eat some simple meals at their resort.

After dinner, they walked beside the ocean. "I wish I had known you when you were young," she said. She looked at him in the moonlight, believing that in the softened light she could catch a glimpse of what he'd looked like as a young man.

"I was much taller when I was young," he said. "And I had a full head of hair. Better eyesight, too." He sighed.

"Actually, I was pretty much exactly the way I am now. But I did have more hair."

"Did you always want to be a bank manager?"

He chuckled. "Does anyone grow up wishing to be a bank manager? I wanted to be a pilot. I thought that would be a glamorous life, and I could travel all over the world. But, flying school cost money and money was tight. So, I did the sensible thing and got a job at the bank and took college at night. I've pretty much always done the sensible thing." He paused and turned to look at her. "Except with you."

"You're not sensible with me?"

He seemed to take her question seriously. He gazed ahead as they walked on. She liked the feel of his hand in hers, the way they'd found a rhythm together as they walked hand in hand. "I don't feel sensible when I'm around you. You have this wonderful joy about you that makes me want to embrace life the way you do, even if it's not sensible."

"I can think of nothing more sensible than embracing life and squeezing every drop from it. The funny thing is, I think I've always been sensible, too, or at least done the expected thing. It was only when I decided to run away from my own family and my own home at Christmas that I ever did anything completely out of the ordinary." She kicked a pebble out of her way. "My family thought I was crazy. And now that I've acted crazy once? I can't seem to stop."

"I like you crazy."

She smiled. "I like me crazy, too."

He didn't talk much about his family. She knew he and his wife had lost one of their two sons to war. He had one grandson with the surviving child. "What about you? Did your son think you were crazy?"

His hand suddenly went rigid. "I suspect my son thinks I'm senile," he said harshly.

And then she got it. She turned to find his face set in rigid lines. She leaned into him, nudging him with her shoulder. "He's suspicious of me, right?"

He stopped walking. Simply stopped, as though her words had halted him in his tracks. "How did you know that?"

She laughed, although in truth she didn't feel very amused. "My son accused me of being a naïve old widow." Okay, she felt a little amusement as she said, "He called you my boy toy."

After a stunned moment, Earl laughed too. "Your boy toy? Did you tell him I've been collecting my pension for a decade?"

"I suppose it's nice that they worry about us. But they seem to have forgotten the fact that old age brings wisdom." The moonlight was like dancing silver ribbons on the surface of the dark water. "You can't blame your son, I suppose. You are still grieving."

"Doesn't make me senile. Or stupid."

"Does he think I'm after your money?"

She knew she was right when his lips thinned in an angry line. "He thinks it's too early for me to date."

"Maybe, he's right."

"No. Sandy, he's not. I can tell you that within a week of the funeral these nice widows and divorcees were showing up with casseroles. Why does recent death cause women to make casseroles? I mean, why not muffins? Or biscuits? But no, it was always casseroles. I swear every one of them contained at least one can of mushroom soup. If I were only interested in finding another woman, I had plenty of opportunities in my own home town."

She'd heard most of this before, when they'd first met, but it was nice to hear him reiterate that she was special.

When they reached their hotel, nerves begin to flutter in her stomach. Would he ask if he could come into her room? Invite her into his? She hoped he didn't ask, because she didn't think she was ready. Not yet.

He grew suddenly serious and as they stood outside her door. "There's something I would like to tell you."

"All right." She dreaded hearing the next words, assuming they would be some version of, 'you're not the only woman I'm seeing' or he'd tell her he had some sort of social disease. Her son Michael had been quick to inform her about the rise in STDs among the senior population.

She had no idea what the senior population was like in most places, but in Tarlo it was a dismal collection. The single older women far outnumbered the men and the few dates Sandy had been on had left her content to be alone.

He seemed hesitant, unsure how to begin, finally he said, "I don't believe in sex outside of marriage."

CHAPTER 5

She'd been so certain he was going to say something completely different, that it took her a moment to make sense of his words. "Oh." Was all she could come up with as she assimilated the facts that he clearly wasn't playing the field and the chances that he had an STD were probably zero.

There was an awkward moment. He seemed to be waiting for her to expand on her one word answer and she had no idea what to say.

Finally, he continued. He looked a little sheepish and he stared down at the ground as he said, "I probably should have explained this to you before we got on the plane. But it's not the sort of thing you can tell a person on the phone."

"No. It's not."

He pulled himself together. Raised his head. He took her hands and looked into her eyes. "I came to my wife with no past, no baggage. I have only ever been with one woman. What I feel for you isn't what I felt for her. This is different, it's an older, wiser man's love. And I wouldn't want to dishonor you, or this, in any way."

She smiled, feeling flattered, disarmed. "Are you a religious man, Earl?"

"I hope I'm a God-fearing Christian. But this is a personal decision."

"Well, thank you for telling me."

When she went to pull away he stopped her by hanging onto her hands. "You're not disappointed are you?"

She drew in a breath. She supposed if he could be so brutally honest, she could afford to be equally open. "Earl, I haven't had sex since before my husband died and he's been gone more than a dozen years now. I think I can survive two more weeks."

He was still holding onto her hands. "I—would it be all right if I kissed you?"

"I think that would be very nice."

And it was.

When he pulled back from her, her voice was husky as she whispered, "Good night."

SANDY HAD ALWAYS BEEN an early riser, and knowing she was in a tropical paradise for the next two weeks had her waking with the dawn. She didn't want to miss a moment.

She showered and dressed and crept to the door connecting her room with Earl's to listen, but it was quiet. She pulled out the small notebook she always carried, and a pen and jotted a list of groceries. It would be nice to have coffee and breakfast things, and maybe some snack foods to keep in the small kitchen.

She let herself out of her room quietly and walked along the beach until she reached the main building and the office. She asked where the closest grocery store was and chatted with the woman behind the counter. She noticed a rack of brochures offering everything from SCUBA tours to fishing to surfing lessons.

"That company is really good," the woman said, seeing Sandy peruse a surfing brochure.

"Oh, I couldn't take up surfing at my age."

"Why not? My dad surfs. He says it keeps him young."

"Your father surfs?"

Sure. Lots of seniors do."

What was she doing, limiting herself like this? She and Earl were strong swimmers. They both loved the water. How dangerous could it be to take a beginner's surf lesson? Before she could stop herself, she'd booked a lesson for that afternoon.

There was a coffee machine in the reception area and she poured two cups. She remembered how Earl liked his coffee and carried the two paper cups back to their condo. When she arrived, she found him sitting outside on the patio table. He smiled at her. "Good morning."

"Morning." She passed him his coffee and sat opposite him.

HE THANKED HER AND SIPPED. She let him get a good hit of caffeine in him before dropping her bombshell. "Earl, I've got a present for you."

"A present?"

"I booked us a surf lesson for this afternoon."

He did not immediately light up with joy. "A surf lesson?"

"Now you're looking at me the way my oldest son looks at me. Like I'm crazy. But the woman in the front office says there are people in their eighties still surfing. Besides, it's a beginner's lesson. What can go wrong?"

He scratched at his cheek. Sipped more coffee. "Drowning, heart attack, shark attack, stroke. I could probably even die of embarrassment."

"I'd rather die learning to surf than sitting in a rocking chair."

"Well, then, I guess somebody better go with you to haul your body back to the mainland."

THEIR SURF INSTRUCTOR was the same age as her oldest grandson. His name was Reggie, and he was deeply tanned with long hair tied back in a ponytail. He called her Sandy and addressed Earl as Pops.

But he didn't tell them they were too old to surf. When she saw the line of surfers hovering out in the deep water on their boards, and watched a couple of them skim across the top of the water, hands held out, feet moving as though they were dancing, she began to think she'd done a very foolish thing. "I'm not sure about this, Reggie."

Reggie followed her gaze and said, "Don't worry, *Tutu wahine*, we won't have you way out there until lesson two."

She laughed and said, "Tutu, what?"

"Means Grandmother in the Hawaiian language."

"You're certainly as cheeky as my grandson. All right, then. Show us what we have to do."

They spent fifteen minutes surfing on sand. They practiced lying down on their boards, pretending to paddle as they pushed their hands in the sand, then they got to their knees. Finally, he showed them how to jump from knees to a squat and then finally, to standing.

"How are your knees feeling, Earl?" she asked after they'd been practicing for a while.

"A little creaky, but fine. Yours?"

"They're okay." Though her hip gave her a little trouble.

When she thought she might need a hip replacement before they ever put their boards in the water, Reggie finally decreed that they were ready. "Check out those waves."

She and Earle turned and watched the breakers rolling in, endlessly, the lithe, young surfers dancing on their crests like mythical creatures.

"Are you sure about this?" Earl asked.

Oh, she was very, very unsure. She looked down at their two pairs of feet, a little wrinkled, with many miles on them. Her pedicure sparkled in the sun and somehow the bright, foolish color gave her courage. She raised her head and looked Earl straight in the eye. "If we don't try surfing now, when do you think we'll ever try it?"

He grinned at her, "Last one in's a rotten egg."

They strapped the tethers around their ankles and walked their boards into the ocean. They didn't bother racing, it was enough work hefting their boards down the beach. Reggie offered to carry hers but she waved him off. She might be old, but if those little kids farther down the beach could carry their own boards she figured she could, too.

Nerves clutched at her stomach as she splashed into the waves. Reggie walked out with them and when they were about waist high he told them to stop. "Remember what you learned up on the beach. Listen to my instructions." He must have read her uncertainty on her face. "You'll be fine. I haven't lost a student yet."

"Okay."

"Who wants to go first?"

"Ladies first," Earl said.

"You being a gentleman or a chicken?" she asked.

He laughed at her. "Both."

"Wish me luck." She hoisted herself up and slithered onto the board face down. It was a lot rockier out here than on the sand.

Reggie held the back of her board. "Okay, I got a nice, small wave coming. Get ready."

She was as ready as she'd ever be. Which was not ready at all. And then he pushed her off. She felt the roll of the wave beneath her, and managed to get to her knees, barely, before the board bucked her like a bronco with a first time rider.

*S*he slipped under the water, and popped up, spluttering and laughing.

Then it was Earl's turn. She watched, saw the concentration in his face. He got one foot planted before he was tossed off too.

They tried again. And again. Every time she tried to get to her feet, she fell off the board. She had water up her nose, in her ears and as she came up laughing and sputtering, she couldn't wait to try again.

To her surprise, Earl was pretty good. By the fourth time, he'd made it to his feet and ridden a wave to the shore. She laughed and clapped.

It took her about five more attempts before all the things she was learning and trying to remember, came together in one magic moment. She felt the wave lift her, jumped from her knees to her feet in an ungainly squat and then, wobbling and swaying like a sapling in strong winds, she started to rise.

"Arms out," Reggie yelled.

She put her arms out, using them to balance. And then she felt as though she were floating. Well, she *was* floating, and the lovely wave gently carried her in.

"Oh, my gosh, I did it. I caught a wave!" She laughed. "Let's do it again!"

She and Earl surfed for the rest of their lesson and then sloshed their way out. She felt waterlogged, sticky with salt and as happy as she'd ever been in her life.

"We did it," she said to Earl. She took his hands and they spun in a circle on the sand. A young family, obviously here for their own lesson, was watching, and when Sandy collapsed on her towel for a rest, the young mom approached her. "You looked like you were having so much fun that I took a few pictures. If you give me your email address, I'll send them to you."

"Oh, that is so nice of you." Sandy recited her email address and the woman tapped it into her phone. She nodded. "Okay, I'm sending them right now."

"I really appreciate it."

"My son was too afraid to try surfing, but when he saw you out there, he decided he could do it, too."

"Tell him he's right. He can do anything he puts his mind to."

They ate fish tacos on the beach and Sandy borrowed the young woman's phone and took photos of her and her family, now being taught by Reggie. The little boy was timid at first, but she had the pleasure of seeing him catch on fast and soon he was unstoppable.

Even though she felt young inside, her body reminded her of her age when they got back to their resort.

They showered and when Earl asked if she wanted to go out for dinner, she groaned. "I am so tired I think I'll sleep for a week. And I'm full from those fish tacos. How about you?"

He looked relieved. "Honestly, I was asking to be polite."

It was only six o'clock so she invited him into her room and they snuggled up on her bed to watch the news. Then they found a fairly recent movie that neither of them had seen. They began watching. Earl put his arm around her and she settled her head on his chest. She could hear his heart beating and smell his aftershave and she was certain she could smell a hint of the ocean on his skin.

"This is nice," he said.

"Mmm."

The movie had barely begun when she felt her eyes grow heavy. She was so comfortable, she didn't even fight her drowsiness.

When she awoke, suddenly, it was dark and she and Earl were sound asleep on top of her bed. She got up, flipped off the TV and then took the spare duvet she'd found earlier in the closet and draped it over the two of them. She didn't even bother undressing, simply snuggled up to Earl and fell back to sleep.

The next time she woke, sun was streaming into the

room and Earl wore the stunned expression of a man who's just woken and doesn't know where he is.

"Good morning," she said.

"Morning." He sat up, looked down at his fully clothed self. "I didn't mean to fall asleep."

"Neither did I. I think we exhausted ourselves yesterday."

She rolled out of bed and stifled a moan. Every muscle in her body ached.

"You know what I'd like to do today?" Earl asked, rolling out of his own side of the bed and looking as stiff as she felt.

"What?" If he said deep sea fishing or hiking, she supposed she'd be a good sport and go along. But the thought of another day of intense physical activity made her groan inside.

"Absolutely nothing," he said.

She laughed. "Let's have a nice lazy morning and then maybe later we'll have enough energy to go shopping."

"Shopping?" He did not look as though shopping topped his list of favorite things to do.

"Yes. I am going to buy you a present. Some new bathing trunks. I think a man who surfs as well as you do, deserves a bathing suit from this millennium.

He was a good sport, and they spent the afternoon poking around the retail establishments. There was a picture-framing place, and that gave her an idea.

She bought him a pair of navy blue bathing trunks and insisted he needed a new pair of beach sandals. Then they bought groceries so they could cook their own dinner that night.

It was nice settling down from the first few days of feeling like they had to do everything at once, to finding a slower rhythm. He barbecued a breast for himself and marinated tofu strips for her, while she put together a salad. For dessert they had fresh papaya and mango. She thought she could eat the fresh tropical fruits forever and always be wowed anew by each bite.

They fell into a routine after that. Days spent walking, swimming and resting. They went out for dinner some nights and cooked at home others. But the best part was that they never ran out of things to talk about.

They even tried surfing one more time.

On their last day, she made an excuse to go into town.

"That's great. I want to go to town too," he said, spoiling her plans for her surprise.

"But I have to do something and you can't come with me."

He nodded, looking very serious. "That's fine, Sandy. I have something to do too and you can't come with me."

It was foolish to make separate trips to town, so they rode down together and when they reached the shopping area, they agreed to meet for coffee in half an hour.

The shopping area was so small it was impossible not to see where each other were headed. They shared a helpless glance. Finally, he said. "I am going to walk into this convenience store right here and purchase a newspaper. Will five minutes give you enough time to disappear?"

"Yes."

"Good. And don't come out of wherever you're going for ten minutes."

"That's an excellent plan." She really did like how good an organizer he was. "But what if we're going to the same place?"

He shrugged. "What will be, will be."

He disappeared into the convenience store, as he'd promised, and she practically ran into the photography and framing store.

"You okay?" the young woman behind the counter asked as she burst inside, wheezing.

"Yes. Sorry, I'm trying to surprise my—" She almost said husband and stopped herself in time. She replaced the word husband with friend. Earl was neither of those things, she realized, but something in between that had no proper name.

"I emailed you some photographs to be printed."

She'd enlisted the help of the resort manager, the nice woman who was usually behind the desk and they'd used her computer to view the photos the young mother had taken of Sandy and Earl learning to surf. Sandy chose three of the five photos the woman had emailed her.

In one, Earl was cruising toward the beach, in fine surfer form. In a second, she'd captured Sandy, she was certain it was when she'd caught her first wave, and while she might not look like a real surfer, she was upright on her board and the expression on her face was exhilarated. Just looking at the photo made Sandy happy all over again.

The third photo she chose was of the two of them doing their happy dance on the beach. They looked like overgrown kids, which in some way, they were.

Sandy had two sets of the photos printed so she could keep one for herself. Earl's set she had framed. She worried a little about the extra bulk in his luggage, but he'd packed like a man with no wife and so he still had plenty of room in his suitcase.

When she'd paid, she crept to the door and peeked out. No sign of Earl so she bolted out of the store and into a gift and souvenir place. There she found a greeting card and a gift bag. She pored over the cards for ages and finally settled on a drawing of a surfer. The caption read *Hang Loose, Dude.*

She'd had the foresight to bring her beach bag with her so Earl would have no idea what she'd purchased. While she was in the souvenir store anyway, she picked up some small gifts for her three sons, her daughters-in-law and her grandchildren. Even though they all thought she was crazy, and told her so, she knew they cared about her and she missed them.

She and Earl were both prompt for their coffee date. He had not had the forethought to bring a big bag along with him. Whatever he'd purchased was small enough to fit into a pocket. She began to feel nervous.

Please, let it not be a ring.

She wasn't ready and Earl certainly wasn't ready. But how could she say no to a man she was falling in love with?

"Are you all right?" he asked.

She took a sip of her latte. "Yes. I hope I didn't get the wrong thing for Katie. That's my granddaughter."

He blinked at her. "You got your grandkids presents?"

She shrugged helplessly. "Small things."

"I never thought. My wife used to do all that." Then he winced. "Sorry, didn't mean to say that."

"It's okay. Would you like me to help you choose something for your grandson?"

"Oh, I would."

They'd decided to enjoy a restaurant dinner for their final night in Hawaii. She wore her prettiest summer dress, a soft black and white wrap dress. He wore linen slacks and a short sleeved gray shirt. They had discovered they preferred to eat early, so it wasn't very crowded in the restaurant and they were given a table that looked out on stunning gardens and the ocean in the background. They both ordered the night's fish special and, as always, both refused coffee afterward since they'd discovered another thing they had in common was that even decaf kept them awake.

They returned to their hotel and Earl said, "Let's go for a walk."

"Wait, I want to give you something first."

"I have something for you, too."

They went into his room, which was identical to hers. "I bought a bottle of champagne," he said, "For our last night. Which seems all wrong. You don't celebrate a sad day."

She leaned in and kissed him. "It's not sad. I'd love some champagne."

She ran back to her room and retrieved the gift bag with the photographs. As she came back into his room, she stopped dead. A jeweler's ring box sat on the table. "Oh, Earl, I..."

"Relax," he said, obviously seeing her distress. "Open it."

Her hands trembled slightly as she ripped off the paper and slowly opened the box. She was almost afraid to look inside, but when she did, she burst out laughing. Exactly as she'd feared, there was a ring inside the box. But not an engagement ring.

It was a silver ring and on the top was a tiny silver hand making the hang loose sign. "Oh, Earl, I love it."

The champagne cork popped and he brought over two glasses of the bubbling liquid. "I thought a Grandma who surfs should have something to remind her every day of how cool she is."

"I'm not cool," she said, accepting the glass.

"You are the coolest person I know." He grew serious, and picking up the box, withdrew the ring. He said, "Do they still have promise rings?"

"I have no idea." It might be old-fashioned, but she liked the idea of a promise ring. He picked up her left hand and glanced at her before pushing the hang loose sign onto her wedding ring finger. She hadn't worn a ring on there for years and the sliding silver felt momentarily strange. "You got the right size," she said, amazed.

"I did." He sounded very pleased with himself.

"A promise ring," she said, looking at the hand pointing at her, thumb and baby finger extended.

"They also call it the Shaka sign," he informed her. "For surfer solidarity everywhere. The promise I make to you is to get to know you better." He was as serious as the ring was foolish. "I didn't think I'd ever feel this way again. And I know we both have families, and homes. I promise to introduce you to my family and my friends. I promise to come to Tarlo, if you'll have me, and get to know your family and friends."

"I accept," she said. Knowing there would be hurdles ahead, but that there was a lot of happiness in her future too.

When she gave him her gift, he studied the photographs, shaking his head. "It's a little like life, isn't it? Most of the time it scoops you up and dumps you on your head. But every once in a while, when you least expect it, life offers you a gift and you catch a wave."

She nodded, understanding him completely.

"When I'm with you," he said, pointing to the photo of them dancing like fools in the sand. "That's how I feel."

She leaned closer to him. "We might be headed into the beach, but our ride isn't over yet. Not nearly."

And then he kissed her.

The best way to keep up with new releases, sales, plus enjoy bonus content and prizes is to join Nancy's newsletter at **nancywarren.net** or join her private Facebook group www.facebook.com/groups/NancyWarrenKnitwits

The Almost Wives Club

An enchanted wedding dress is a matchmaker in this series of romantic comedies where five runaway brides find out who the best men really are!

The Almost Wives Club: **Kate**

Secondhand Bride

Bridesmaid for Hire

The Wedding Flight

If the Dress Fits

The Almost Wives Club Boxed Set

Take a Chance series

Meet the Chance family, a cobbled together family of eleven kids who are all grown up and finding their ways in life and love.

Kiss a Girl in the Rain Take a Chance, Book 1

Iris in Bloom Take a Chance, Book 2

Blueprint for a Kiss Take a Chance, Book 3

Every Rose Take a Chance, Book 4

Love to Go Take a Chance, Book 5

The Sheriff's Sweet Surrender Take a Chance Book 6

The Daisy Game Take a Chance Book 7

Chance Encounter Prequel

Take a Chance Box Set (Prequel and Books 1-3)

The Vampire Knitting Club

Paranormal Cozy Mysteries. When Lucy inherits her grandmother's knitting shop in Oxford, she discovers secrets and solves murders with the help of some special undead amateur sleuths.

The Vampire Knitting Club - Book 1

Stitches and Witches - Book 2

Crochet and Cauldrons - Book 3

Stockings and Spells - Book 4

Purls and Potions - Book 5

Fair Isle and Fortunes - Book 6

Lace and Lies - Book 7

Bobbles and Broomsticks - Book 8

Popcorn and Poltergeists - Book 9

Garters and Gargoyles - Book 10

Diamonds and Daggers - Book 11

Cat's Paws and Curses a Holiday Whodunnit

Vampire Knitting Club Boxed Set 1-3

Vampire Knitting Club Boxed Set 4-6

The Vampire Book Club

A middle aged witch gets sent to Ireland to run an unusual book shop.

The Vampire Book Club - Book 1

Chapter and Curse - Book 2

A Spelling Mistake - Book 3

The Great Witches Baking Show

The Great Witches Baking Show - Book 1

Baker's Coven - Book 2

A Rolling Scone - Book 3

A Bundt Instrument - Book 4

Blood, Sweat and Tiers - Book 5

Toni Diamond Mysteries

Toni is a successful saleswoman for Lady Bianca Cosmetics in this series of humorous cozy mysteries. Along with having an eye for beauty and a head for business, Toni's got a nose for trouble and she's never shy about following her instincts, even when they lead to murder.

Frosted Shadow Toni Diamond Mysteries, Book One

Ultimate Concealer Toni Diamond Mysteries, Book Two

Midnight Shimmer Toni Diamond Mysteries, Book Three

A Diamond Choker For Christmas A Toni Diamond Mysteries Novella

For a complete list of books, check out Nancy's website at nancywarren.net

ABOUT THE AUTHOR

Nancy Warren is the USA Today Bestselling author of more than 100 novels. She's originally from Vancouver, Canada, though she tends to wander and has lived in England, Italy and California at various times. Favorite moments include being the answer to a crossword puzzle clue in Canada's National Post newspaper, being featured on the front page of the New York Times when her book Speed Dating launched Harlequin's NASCAR series, and being nominated three times for Romance Writers of America's RITA award. She's an avid hiker, loves chocolate and most of all, loves to hear from readers! The best way to stay in touch is to sign up for Nancy's newsletter at www.nancywarren.net or join her private facebook group www.facebook.com/groups/NancyWarrenKnitwits .

To learn more about Nancy and her books
www.nancywarren.net

www.ingramcontent.com/pod-product-compliance
Lightning Source LLC
Chambersburg PA
CBHW071233170626
46809CB00008BA/3037